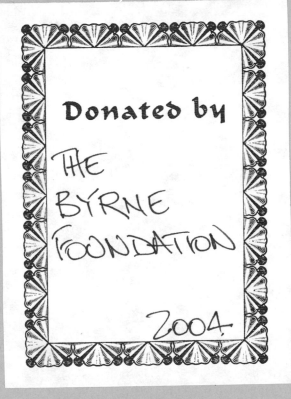

The Several Lives of Orphan Jack

The Several Lives of
Orphan Jack

❋ ❋ ❋

SARAH ELLIS

•

Pictures by
BRUNO ST-AUBIN

A GROUNDWOOD BOOK
DOUGLAS & McINTYRE
TORONTO VANCOUVER BERKELEY

Groundwood Books / Douglas & McIntyre
720 Bathurst Street, Suite 500, Toronto, Ontario M5S 2R4

Distributed in the USA by Publishers Group West
1700 Fourth Street, Berkeley, CA 94710

We acknowledge for their financial support of our publishing
program the Canada Council for the Arts, the Government of Canada
through the Book Publishing Industry Development Program
(BPIDP), the Ontario Arts Council and the Government of Ontario
through the Ontario Media Development Corporation's
Ontario Book Initiative.

ONTARIO ARTS COUNCIL
CONSEIL DES ARTS DE L'ONTARIO

National Library of Canada Cataloging in Publication
Ellis, Sarah
The several lives of Orphan Jack / by Sarah Ellis; pictures by Bruno
St-Aubin.
ISBN 0-88899-529-6 (bound). ISBN 0-88899-618-7 (pbk).
I. St-Aubin, Bruno II. Title.
PS8559.L57S49 2003   jC813'.54   C2003-901284-0
PZ7

Library of Congress Control Number: 2003102599

Printed and bound in Canada

For Mike and Chris

Be tramps.

— THE MOUSE AND HIS CHILD

Chapter One

"GENTLEMEN!"

Schoolmaster Bane slapped his pointer down on his desk and barked out a question. "What is the purpose of snow?"

The question floated out into the dead air of the classroom and over the bowed heads of the boys. Then it gave up hope and began to sink toward the floor.

"Edwin!"

Edwin heaved himself out of his desk and stood in the aisle. An answer surfaced in his head, and he gave it with a sure sense of defeat. Edwin had answers, but they were never the right answers.

"Snowballs, sir?"

Slap! The desk took another lashing from the pointer.

"No, you scurvy lump of a semiwitted ne'er-do-well. Sit! Hugo!"

A bullet of chalk whizzed down the aisle and connected with the ear of the dozing Hugo.

"Ow! Zanzibar, sir?" Once, long ago, Hugo had been right with the answer "Zanzibar," and he lived in hope of repeating his victory.

"No, you booby-brained mutton-head. Otherjack!"

Otherjack stood up. Two roads lay before him and both led to trouble. Give the wrong answer and Mr. Bane might reach the end of his rope and get out the strap. Mr. Bane had a very short rope. Answer the question correctly and Edwin, the late-night basher, would get him after dark.

Ah, well, Otherjack said to himself. Better the trouble that lies around the corner than the trouble staring you in the face.

"The purpose of snow is to keep plants warm in winter and to brighten our gloomy evenings, sir."

"Correct." Mr. Bane sounded disappointed. He turned his pale blue eyes to the book in his hand, *Little Truths for the Instruction of Boys*.

"What is the purpose of… "

A timid knock at the door saved the boys from further little truths.

"Enter!"

A small warty boy put his head around the door. "Otherjack to Dr. Keen, sir."

Breathing stopped all over the room. A summons to the headmaster could cause many a stomach to come loose from its moorings.

Otherjack stood up looking calm as a pudding.

Otherjack's friend Marcus, sitting in the desk behind him, gave him a sympathetic punch between the shoulder blades. Edwin abandoned his plans for a bashing.

But Otherjack stood up looking calm as a pudding.

Otherjack was the king of staying out of trouble. In all his twelve years, in all the twelve years he had lived at the Opportunities School for Orphans and Foundlings, he had never once been flogged. Otherjack had skipped over trouble, danced around trouble, slid under trouble, melted away from trouble, talked his way out of trouble and slipped between two close troubles like a cat through a picket fence.

He did not mean to break his record now.

He walked down the hall toward the headmaster's study, running his finger along the mustard-colored wall and breathing deeply to keep his stomach in place. The ghost smells of years of boiled turnip dinners kept pace with him.

He sifted through his list of useful words.

Trepidation, that was it. Like fear, but less so.

He came to the headmaster's door, so smooth and shiny and dark brown that he wanted to lick it. He knocked.

Turnips, trouble and trepidation, he said to himself. That's the life of an Opportunities Boy.

Chapter Two

"COME!"

Otherjack turned the crystal doorknob and pushed open the heavy door.

Dr. Keen's office was as solemn as church. The headmaster leaned forward across his big desk. His long pale fingers were arranged like a tent in front of his chin. Otherjack stared at Dr. Keen's fingernails and thought of baby Myrtle, the latest foundling left on the school steps. Only babies and Dr. Keen had fingernails that clean.

"Well, young man, this is your moment of Opportunity."

Otherjack's heart did a leapfrog. He hadn't wanted to let himself hope. The "opportunity" at the Opportunities School for Orphans and Foundlings was that at age twelve each student was sent out to learn a trade. At twelve he could leave behind Mr. Bane and Mr. Hector and Mr. Wormwood. At twelve he could leave behind grammar and deportment and the purpose of snow. At twelve he could go out into the world in a new set of clothes and be Somebody.

"We have found you an apprenticeship with a firm of bookkeepers. Fine old firm. You are a very fortunate boy indeed."

Bookkeepers! Otherjack felt a bubble of excitement begin to bounce around inside him. Bookkeepers must be the people who keep books safe.

He looked beyond Dr. Keen to a glass-fronted bookcase behind him. Thick leather spines — brown, red and green.

Dr. Keen's voice floated away, and Otherjack began to imagine. A room full of books, floor to ceiling. Colors like jewels, and gold words inviting you in. And the keeper, sitting at the door in a tidy uniform, keeping the books safe, dry and warm.

And reading! Of course there would be reading. All those ideas sitting sideways on shelves just waiting for him. Stories and adventures and books with pictures of elephants and Zanzibar and the wonders of the world and a whole dictionary and...

Dr. Keen's voice invaded his daydream.

" ...inclined to inattention but good with sums. And we expect, of course, that you will always keep the good name of the Opportunities School for Orphans and Foundlings uppermost in your mind. Any questions?"

Otherjack had nothing but questions. Would scholars come to use the books and did the bookkeeper help them find things? Did a bookkeeper mend the books if they were damaged? What would happen if some scoundrel tried to steal the books?

But Otherjack knew, from his years of keeping out of trouble, that when Dr. Keen said, "Any questions?" the only good answer was "No, sir."

"No, sir."

"Fine. Then your apprenticeship begins tomorrow. Young Gus will take over your house job in the scullery. Lady Duff from the Benevolents will meet you in your dormitory after tea."

Otherjack felt like turning a cartwheel right there in Dr. Keen's office. What was the word?

Euphoria. Like happy, but more so.

Bookkeeping! Bookkeeping was going to be glorious! Otherjack had a vision of himself racing down the road, blowing on a policeman's whistle, in pursuit of some villain who had stolen a book.

Scholars and scoundrels. Volumes and villains. That will be my life, said Otherjack to himself. That will be the life of a bookkeeper's apprentice.

Chapter Three

LADY DUFF placed her bony beringed fingers on her large front and gazed at Otherjack.

"Well I remember the day you arrived, a poor wee orphan. All you had was a name. And didn't the school already have a poor wee orphan called Jack? So they named you Otherjack. Dr. Keen is so clever." Lady Duff gave a merry laugh. "And here you are, about to be apprenticed. What a lucky lad. I'm sure you know how lucky you are. Do you?"

Otherjack nodded.

"Of course you do. To be apprenticed to Ledger and Ledger. A fine old firm. It is all Dr. Keen's doing, Dr. Keen's connections. I'm sure you're very grateful. Are you very grateful?"

Otherjack nodded.

"Of course you are. My dear father, of blessed memory, long since passed over, had some business with Ledger and Ledger."

As Lady Duff talked, she pulled clothes out of a box and held them against Otherjack.

"Just try on this coat."

Otherjack slid his arms into a hairy brown jacket. It was made out of some stuff you could use to scour pots. His wrists hung out of the sleeves like spare parts.

Lady Duff pulled the sleeves down firmly. "This will do very nicely. Lots of wear left in this coat. Can't have you disgracing us at Ledger and Ledger, can we? Now, what about trousers?"

She knelt down to measure a pair of trousers against Otherjack's legs.

His first long pants. Oh, magnificent day! Magnificent. Like good, but more so.

Otherjack stared down at Lady Duff's hat. It was decorated with a pheasant feather. The ladies of the Benevolent Ladies Auxiliary to the Opportunities School for Orphans and Foundlings were known as the Benevolents, and they all wore hats. When he was a little boy, Otherjack thought that benevolent meant something to do with hats. But then he found out it meant knitting and collecting things that were too worn, broken, old or stained for regular children, but would do for orphans and foundlings.

Most of the boys mocked the Benevolents. A favorite trick was to stuff a pillow down the front of your shirt and pretend to be Lady Duff and then make rude noises. But Otherjack had a reason to think well of the auxiliary.

At Christmas each student at the Opportunities School was given a pair of socks and a present. The Christmas Otherjack was ten, the Benevolents had given him a dictionary. It was grubby and missing the first part so that it didn't have any A or B words, but from C to Z it had given Otherjack some of his happiest moments. The words were always there, ready to be taken out and used or just examined. A sunrise was better when you knew the word sublime. Oatmeal for dinner was somehow not so sad when you knew the word mingy. A bashing from Edwin was not so horrible when you could secretly call him a vandal.

Best of all, the other boys could not steal or spoil Otherjack's words. They were his secret hoard.

Lady Duff snapped a pair of trousers in the air and folded them smartly. "Do you have your cap, then?"

Otherjack nodded and pulled his orange- and blue-striped Opportunities cap out of his pocket.

"Excellent. I'm sure you will be a credit to the school. Are you determined to be a credit to the school?"

Otherjack nodded.

Lady Duff took Otherjack by the shoulders and held him in front of her. "Of course you are. Just remember this. With diligence, fortitude and the will to succeed, any boy can rise above his... er... unfortunate beginnings. Are you that boy?"

Otherjack tried to arrange his face into a combination of lucky, grateful, a credit to the school, formerly unfortunate and someone about to rise. It took a lot of arranging, and he wasn't quite sure what to do with his eyebrows.

He nodded. "Yes, ma'am. Thank you, ma'am."

Lady Duff left in a wave of floral perfume and benevolence. Otherjack laid his clothes out on the bed.

Pants and possibilities, he said to himself. That's the life of a Somebody.

Chapter Four

OTHERJACK stood with his hands in the sink. Floating islands of grease formed and reformed on the surface of the cold dishwater. A roasting pan, blackened and crusty, poked out of the few remaining soap suds like a freighter run aground.

Otherjack was not concentrating on the dishes. Neither was Gus, the small freckled boy who stood at the other end of the shallow stone sink. Gus was holding a grubby, sopping tea towel and hanging onto Otherjack's every word like a limpet.

"Here's what you need to know about being a scullery boy," said Otherjack. "When Cook's been drinking, he goes angry or he goes sad."

Gus nodded. "When he goes angry he beats the scullery boy, don't he, Otherjack? I heard."

"That's it. Wooden spoon, soup ladle, frying pan. Whatever comes to hand."

Gus pulled the tea towel over his head and groaned. "Why was I chosen as the new scullery boy? I could have done washing. I could have done fires. I could have done chamber pots. Anything!"

Otherjack uncovered Gus's head. "Don't get yourself in a swivet. You'll be fine because I'm going to tell you the secret. Are you paying attention?"

Gus gave a sniffy nod.

"The secret is to make Cook go sad."

"What's he do then?" said Gus.

"He cries. Huge big tears, and his nose runs something terrible. Sometimes it drips into the soup. Then he sits in his chair and goes to sleep. Come over here. You can hear him snoring now."

The boys went to the door that led from the scullery into the kitchen and opened it a crack. The sound of a bear growling was followed by the sound of a steam whistle.

Otherjack pulled Gus back to the sink.

"So if he cries there's no beating?" said Gus.

"Neither smack nor whack nor clip nor clout."

Gus took a deep breath. "What makes Cook sad, then?"

"Talking about the sea," said Otherjack. "Cook was born by the sea. He makes it sound lovely. He says that the water is never the same color twice. He says that storms leave treasures behind. He told me he once saw a mermaid. Sometimes he sings.

Always the same song about the call of the tide and his sea-wracked heart."

"How do you get him started?"

Otherjack pulled out the roasting pan and held it up dripping. "You just need to ask him a question. You can say, 'Cook, were you ever in a terrible storm?' or 'How do you fix a leaky boat?' or 'By the way, what's the biggest sea creature you ever saw?'"

"Storm. Boat. Creature." Gus was frowning. "I think I can remember. Who told you the secret, Otherjack?"

"Nobody. It was my own idea."

"You must be clever," said Gus. "I'm not clever. Storm. Boat. Creature. Does it always work?"

Otherjack sighed and turned back to the sink. "No. Nothing always works. Some days Cook cannot be turned away from his anger. But one knock a week is better than a beating a day. Just remember, slops and slaps is the life of a scullery boy, but so is stories."

Gus nodded and flapped his tea towel in the air. "Slops and slaps and stories. I'll remember. Thank you, Otherjack."

Chapter Five

"HANDS!"

Mr. Ledger, of Ledger and Ledger, bent his head over Otherjack's outstretched hands.

Crow, thought Otherjack, looking at Mr. Ledger's sleek, black, shiny hair. Not a feather out of place.

"Disgraceful! Wash, boy! And don't dawdle. Time is money here at Ledger and Ledger and we *do not dawdle*!" Mr. Ledger spoke in little explosions.

Otherjack went into the gentlemen's cloakroom and washed his hands with unusual energy. The water grew dirtier but his hands stayed about the same color. How could time be money? Money was heavy and made a clinking sound, and you kept it in your pocket or in a treasure chest. Time was light and quiet, and you couldn't keep it at all.

"Boy!" Mr. Ledger led Otherjack to a high desk. On the desk sat a large book, a pen and a bottle of ink.

Finally, thought Otherjack. It's time to read.

But when the book was flipped open, it contained no words at all. Only numbers.

Mr. Ledger ran his pale waxy fingers up and down.

"Columns," he said. He ran his finger back and forth.

"Rows," he said.

"Add," he said.

Otherjack liked numbers. He liked eight because eight is like snowman. He liked four because four is like a mean little girl with blond pigtails and pointed elbows. He liked the tumbling twins, six and nine. And he had figured out arithmetic for the same reason he learned everything at the Opportunities School — to avoid getting into trouble.

But when Otherjack began to add, these numbers would not behave themselves at all. The rows and columns just would not add up to the same total. They wouldn't even be wrong in the same way twice.

Minute after minute, hour after hour. The ink crept up Otherjack's fingers. The tidy page grew muckier and muckier. Every time he looked up, he was being glared at by Mr. Ledger. The only sound was the scratching of pens. The numbers piled up in Otherjack's head like potato peelings in a slop pail. They crowded out words. They crowded out plans and ideas. They crowded out thinking altogether.

Fourteen plus twenty-three equals thirty-seven,

*The numbers piled up in Otherjack's head
like potato peelings in a slop pail.*

carry the three. Otherjack carried the three. Gleeful three was overjoyed to jump over a column. Otherjack's eyes were sliding shut. The scratching of pens was joined by the sound of a fly buzzing against the window.

Two of the bookkeepers happened to meet and pause close to Otherjack's desk.

Words! He was hungry for words. He could not help eavesdropping.

" ...adjust the partner's account in the case of the dissolved partnership... examine the disputed account... report for the arbiter... "

Arbiter. Otherjack ran the word around in his mouth. What does an arbiter do? If a drinker drinks, then an arbiter must arbit.

"Boy!"

Mr. Ledger's crow voice cawed right in Otherjack's ear. Otherjack jumped and clutched the book in front of him. The book shifted and knocked over the ink pot. A river of black ran down the page of numbers, off the edge of the page, off the edge of the desk, as Otherjack watched, paralyzed.

Mr. Ledger was very loud and then he was very quiet. When he was loud he told Otherjack that he was the most useless, bone-headed dullard that they had ever had the misfortune to employ as an apprentice. Then he was quiet and pulled a small black accounts book out of his pocket and did some fast arithmetic.

"Eleven weeks' wages," said Mr. Ledger. "That is the sum of what you now owe us."

As Otherjack trudged back to school, his day's work ended, a light rain began to fall. His hand was cramped, his eyes burned and his brain was numb. Mr. Ledger's scornful voice rang in his ears. With every step he recited a day of the week, a month of the year, and then the years themselves. More numbers. Endless combinations of the same ten things.

This was it? This was his Opportunity? A brain full of arithmetic and no room for a single dream?

Sums, sameness and scorn, said Otherjack to himself. That's the life of a Ledger lad.

Chapter Six

OTHERJACK lay on his narrow bed and stared at his inky fingers in the moonlight. Sleep was as far away as Zanzibar. He reached for the familiar comfort of his dictionary and began to flip through its pages. Then he slapped the book down on the blanket.

What was the use of a dictionary without B's? What was the use of a dictionary that didn't warn you about bookkeeping?

Seven years. That's how long an apprenticeship lasted. By the time he left Ledger and Ledger he would be an old man of nineteen with a brain as tight as a sausage stuffed with sums and a spirit as small and hard as a dried pea.

He lay listening to the breathing of the boys around him in the dormitory. Cold stale air moving from bed to bed, boy to boy. In and out of Edwin, in and out of Alfie, in and out of Michael, in and out of Marcus.

It could be worse, he said to himself, thinking of Rupert. Rupert was apprenticed to a surgeon. His Opportunity was all bones and blood, and one of his jobs was to collect leeches.

Or he could be Harold, who was apprenticed to a blacksmith. Once he got a bad burn that made him weep in the night and left an ugly, shiny, puckered patch on his arm.

Otherjack could stay out of trouble. He could make the best of it.

Suddenly a voice interrupted his thoughts. This voice was loud and bold and bossy. It came from somewhere near Otherjack's stomach.

You're trapped!

"What?"

It's your life!

"But... "

Go! Just go!

"How could I... ?"

Run away!

"I can't. Remember when Rupert tried? They'll find me and fetch me back and flog me. Besides, where could I... ?"

The sea, of course! the sea!

The sea. Otherjack remembered Cook's stories. The sea that lives where the sun comes up. Birds fishing and wild waves and the way the water breathes at the turn of the tide.

"But when... ?"

RUN AT DAWN!

Otherjack's feet hit the cold floor before he knew he had made a decision. He pulled his box from under his bed. He spared a kind thought for Lady Duff as he laid his second-best shirt out on the floor.

Two shirts. One to wear and one to bundle. On the shirt he arranged his dictionary, now forgiven, his pre-Opportunity trousers and his Benevolent socks.

LUNCH!

Oh, yes. He hadn't eaten his lunchtime buns and cheese, because he had spent his break scrubbing ink off his desk. He added them to the small pile.

Carefully he folded and tied the shirt, turning the sleeves into a handle. Then he dressed and sat on the floor, leaning back against the bed, clutching his bundle and waiting for the first hint of dawn through the high dormitory window.

Boldness and bundles, he said to himself. That's the life of an ex-bookkeeper.

Two shirts. One to wear and one to bundle.

Chapter Seven

EVERYTHING was too loud. The creak of the third stair. The comments of the kitchen cat. The screech of the door latch. The beating of Otherjack's heart.

Outside he huddled close to the corner of the brick wall and stared down the drive — the long straight drive. No curve or bush to hide an escaping boy.

The sky lightened from pewter to silver.

Otherjack's staying-out-of-trouble voice had a quiet comment.

"Usually we stays where we're put."

Somewhere a window slid open.

We DON'T STAY! WE RUN!

Otherjack's stomach issued the command and together they leapt five giant crunching steps over the gravel drive and onto the grass. Running, Otherjack felt eyes drilling into his back, and with every gasping step he expected to hear the voice of Keen or Bane, the voice of discovery. Half slipping on the dewy lawn, he sprinted toward the front gate. Minutes that felt like hours later he slid between its iron railings, unnoticed. Turning, he took one deep breath and one last look at the staring windows of the school as they turned pink in the dawn.

"The sea is where the sun comes up." The road to the left was patched with light and shadow.

Come along here, it said. I know you. I have trees. I will hide you.

But the road straight ahead, wide and open, ended in the rising sun. So, feeling like the only upright thing in a flat world, Otherjack set off.

Conspicuous, he said to himself. Like sticking out, but more so.

Holding his bundle over his shoulder, he began to trot. He was the only thing moving. He glanced over his shoulder. The school seemed as big and near as ever. A gull screamed overhead, and Otherjack's stomach tried to jump out his throat.

FASTER!

Otherjack obeyed, pausing only to take off his jacket and tie it around his waist. At every step he expected to feel a heavy hand clamping onto his shoulder.

Field after bare field, their crops harvested.

Finally he saw the beginning of low scrubby green. A wood. Safety. A final sprint took him deep into shade and cover.

Shade, cover, one deep breath and...

WHERE'S BREAKFAST?

Otherjack was just swinging his bundle over his shoulder to look into the possibility of breakfast when he heard it. The sound of hoofbeats. He glanced back into the bright sun and saw a small shape on the road. Small but getting bigger.

He imagined early morning at the school. An unmade bed, an empty place at breakfast.

He was discovered.

HIDE!

Otherjack threw himself headfirst into the bushes at the side of the path. Ow! Not bushes but brambles. They tore at his clothes, his bundle. The hoofbeats were louder. He pushed his way into the snarly, grabbing thicket and fell through on the other side. He took half a breath of relief before he felt an unusual airiness around his ears.

His cap.

He peered back through the leaves. There it was, bright orange and blue, beyond reach. It might as well have been a sign saying, "Opportunities Boy This Way." And the hoofbeats were getting louder.

The hedge was taller than Otherjack, and there was a narrow dirt track along its inside edge.

RUN!

No point, said Otherjack. A horse is faster than a boy and a man on a horse is taller than a hedge.

Just then Otherjack heard the hollow *plonk-plonk* of many bells, and around the corner of the path

appeared a herd of sheep — a white river of wool
and feet. Following them was a shepherd, smiling
and smoking a pipe.

"Otherjack!" a voice bellowed from beyond the
hedge.

DIVE!

With one startled glance at the shepherd,
Otherjack dropped his bundle and launched himself
in among the sheep. He crouched down, and their
soft strong bodies closed over the top of him.
Waddling like a duck, he moved along with them.

"Here! You!" It was the familiar voice of Bane.
"Seen a lad pass this way?"

There was the bubbling sound of a pipe being
sucked. "Lad?"

"Yes, *lad.*"

"What sort of lad?"

"The plain sort, you loblolly. Stripling, tow-
headed. Have you seen him?"

There was a pause. Otherjack's knees began to
burn, and he abandoned his duck walk and fell to
crawling. He grabbed onto the sheep in front of him
and knee-walked along, narrowing his eyes against
the puffing dust and trying to ignore the smell of
back end of sheep.

"Can't say I've seen such a one come this way,"
said the shepherd.

"Pah! What good are you then? Good day to
you." Otherjack heard the horse whinny.

He abandoned his duck walk and fell to crawling.

"Did see such a one elsewhere, though," said the shepherd thoughtfully.

"Well, why didn't you say so at once? *Where*, you numble-gut?"

Otherjack and his sheep escort party moved out of earshot.

Some minutes later the sheep-river halted.

"Come on out then, you bleatincheat," said a laughing voice.

Otherjack stood up and drank in a deep breath of lovely air. Then he made his way to the bank of the sheep-river.

"What was that you called me?"

"Bleatincheat. Sheep, by another name. I'm Gabriel. Are you the Otherjack that yon bacon-face was bothered about?"

"Yes." Otherjack paused.

Was he Otherjack? He had made his great escape. He had been clever and quick. He wasn't Other anything.

"But I'm really just Jack. Thank you for hiding me."

"Well, my fine black-faced ladies did the hiding. All I did was spin a tale." Gabriel sucked on his pipe, peered into its depths and then put it in his pocket. "Bacon-face is on his way north, by the way. You'd best stay clear of those parts. On a flit, are you?"

"Yes. I've run away from school and I'm off to the sea. But they are trying to fetch me back."

"Happy to help, then. I've been on a flit my own self once upon a time. And in this old world I'm more for the flitters than the fetchers." Gabriel gave Jack a mighty pat on the back. "Good luck to you, Jack. Cheerio." The plonk of bells began again as the river started to move.

Jack slapped the dust from his clothes, gave a big sneeze and went back to collect his bundle. He pushed his way back through the hedge and picked up his cap. He stuck it in his pocket. No point traveling the roads as a marked man.

For the rest of the day Jack walked. Brown field, green field, flowered wood and rocky hill. It was the most ordinary and the most extraordinary thing he had done in his whole trouble-slipping life. He stuck a stick through the sleeves of his shirt bundle and balanced it over his shoulder. It bounced with every step.

With every step he left a little bit of Otherjack behind in the dust. No bells, no rules, no masters. His shadow followed him and then he followed his shadow as he made his way toward the sea. He skipped and danced and strolled and knew without a glimmer of a doubt that he could do it. He could walk anywhere. To the sea. To Zanzibar. To the rest of his life.

Flitters and fetchers and friends, said Jack to himself. That's the life of a wandering boy.

Chapter Eight

AT DUSK Jack came to a patch of blackberries. The berries were as fat and sweet as jam. He picked and ate, picked and ate. Dessert is before dinner in the dictionary, he said to himself, so why not in life? Dinner was a bun and cheese and then he had dessert all over again until he was purple and yawning with contentment.

SLEEP!

Jack looked around. The blackberry patch made a very good kitchen but a very poor bedroom. He thought of his bed at school — a hard straw mattress, a thin scratchy blanket that smelled of dust. It wasn't a good bed but at least you could count on it being there every night.

Haystack? Hollow stump? Abandoned hut? Jack walked on into the growing darkness, but he saw none of these.

Finally, in the last glimmer of daylight, he spied a large chestnut tree in the middle of a field. It looked thick and safe.

The tree turned out to be made for climbing, with sturdy branches like a ladder. Jack tied his bundle around his waist and climbed until he reached a pair of broad branches arranged like an armchair. He pulled off his boots. The bundle became a pillow, and the last thing Jack saw before he dropped into sleep was a single star winking through the green hands of leaves above him.

*   *   *

He woke up in thin daylight with the wisps of a dream and no idea where he was. Dripping ink, sheep singing sea shanties. He pulled his scattered thoughts together.

For the first morning of his life he had woken up, not to the loud clanging of the dormitory bell and the rebreathed air of twenty boys, but to sunshine, new air and his own plan.

He tossed his boots and bundle to the base of the tree, then slid off his branch until he was hanging by two hands. He swung back and forth — a monkey or a pendulum or an acrobat. Then, with a whoop, he dropped to the ground.

A second later he was gasping with pain. His feet were burning. He peeled off his socks to investigate. A day of tramping in Opportunities boots had left his feet a sorry mess, with raw bleeding patches and shiny pink blisters.

How could he walk? Unlacing his boots until they were gaping wide, he tried to slide his feet into them. But every crack in the boots, every rough place, every sticking-up nail made his feet burn with pain.

Water would help. Jack remembered the stone bridge he had crossed the night before, not too far away. He tied his boots together and put them around his neck and set off barefoot. The soft cool dust of the road eased his slow limp to the stream.

He slid down the grassy bank and dunked his feet into the cool water.

Aaaaah.

BREAKFAST!

Jack slurped up a big drink of water and then took out the last of his food. One bun, rather stale. One apple. He ate them slowly, making the most of each chew. He peered into the lazy stream. Those feet, bloody and blistered, were not going to take him anywhere soon.

Water. Blackberries. How would he find anything else to eat? A small worm of fear began to wriggle inside him.

He picked up his dictionary and began to flip.

Vicissitude. A change in fortune.

He flopped back onto the grass and let his eyes fall shut.

"Traveling?"

Opening his eyes, Jack saw a face peering over the edge of the bridge — a wrinkled, brown, bearded face with the halo of a grubby leather hat brim.

"Why, yes," said Jack. "I am."

"Where?" said the face.

"The sea," said Jack.

"Fair?" said the face.

Jack was mystified. Was *what* fair? It seemed easiest to just say yes.

"Come," said the face and disappeared.

Jack scooped up his things and scrambled up the bank to see a rickety cart full of pumpkins. Hitched to the cart was a horse wearing a straw hat. The face of few words was holding the reins. He gave Jack a glance, clicked his tongue to the horse and gestured with his thumb over his shoulder.

As the cart began to roll away, Jack pulled himself up over the back and tumbled into the pumpkins. He wriggled his way around the lumps and found a spot where he could lie down. He stared at the deep blue sky with its smear of thin white cloud, even now being polished away by the sun. The wheels squeaked, the harness creaked, the horse whinnied, and Jack gave himself up to the pleasure of being still and moving at the same time.

As the day woke up, the road came to life. Walkers appeared with baskets and barrows. A woman with a big white bundle on her head, a skinny girl herding a

*Jack pulled himself up over the back
and tumbled into the pumpkins.*

skinny goat, a man pushing a mysterious stone wheel, a boy with a set of bagpipes on his back.

They all seemed to know the pumpkin man.

"Good morning, Abe."

"Off to Aberbog, are you?"

"Grand weather for it."

"'day," said Abe, raising his hand just once.

Larger carts and wagons with lively horses edged by as they creaked down the dusty road. A caravan in bright rainbow colors turned in from a crossroad and lumbered ahead of Abe's cart. A green parrot screeched in a cage that swung from a hook above its back door.

At first Jack tried to hide, in case there were searchers on the road. But there was too much to notice in the stream of people that eddied around them. Besides, he reasoned, a young man in search of his fortune does not cower in the bottom of a cart, listening to his stomach rumbling and pretending to be a pumpkin. He looks around boldly to see what the world has to offer.

Jack dusted himself off and sat up tall and proud on the pumpkin pile.

He began to notice stone markers at the side of the road. Aberbog 3. Aberbog 2. Aberbog 1.

Then he smelled it. Fishy and salty and wet.

The smell of the sea. He gulped it in and called out to the solid back in front of him.

"Are we nearly there? Are we nearly at the sea?"

Abe nodded.

Around the next curve in the road, the cart creaked to a halt at the top of the hill, and there it was.

Gray and green and white. Flat and huge. In the near distance a tidy town and beyond it the sea. Waves, sails and no end to it.

"He didn't tell me," said Jack. "Cook didn't tell me that it made you big inside just to look at it. Bigger than big. Vast."

Abe clicked to his horse and they started down the hill. Jack balanced on his pumpkin seat and stared and stared, at sky and sea and the dancing gulls.

Views, vicissitudes and vastness, he said to himself. That's the life of a bird of passage.

Chapter Nine

THE SIGHT of town gave Abe's horse new enthusiasm, and in a few minutes they were there, clopping along a cobbled road to the town square. All around the edge of the square there was a flurry of unloading. One of Abe's carefully hoarded words suddenly made sense to Jack.

Of course!

Fair. A town fair.

Abe edged the cart into an empty space, swung around and stepped in among the pumpkins.

"Down," he said to Jack.

Jack jumped out of the cart and took the pumpkins as Abe handed them down to him, creating a neat pile on the ground. When the cart was empty, Abe reached into an inside pocket of one of his layers of coats and brought out a piece of bread and an onion.

"Eat," he said, handing them to Jack. Then he grabbed a bucket from under the seat and loped off toward the fountain at the center of the square.

Jack sat on the largest pumpkin and dined.

About blinking time, said his stomach.

Never was a sultan at a feast a happier man than Jack with his lunch. The chew of the bread, the crunch of the onion. Jack made it a four-course meal. Bread. Onion. Bread and onion. Onion and bread. And never was a sultan's entertainment more lively than what met Jack's eyes as he looked around the square.

Here was a shoemaker unpacking pairs of glossy brown boots. There was a woman arranging jars of spices on a square of carpet. Jack heard the screech of a parrot and spied the caravan from the road. Two children were hanging shiny pots and pans along its sides. Baskets appeared with mountains of potatoes, beets, apples and squash. Strings of onions hung from poles. Jars of jelly glowed in the sun.

A man walked by with lengths of ribbon and lace fluttering from every part of his clothing. There was yelling and hammering, babies crying and young men whistling, the sound of a flute and the complaining of chickens.

From behind a rack of sheep fleeces came a voice so loud that it cut through all the other sounds.

"Buns, buns, buns! One a penny, get 'em hot. Buns, buns, buns!"

A skinny girl appeared carrying a wooden tray around her neck.

"Buns, buns, buns!"

Jack stared. He couldn't believe that huge voice came from that skinniness. She wandered over close to Jack and leaned against the pumpkin cart while she fished a stone out of her sandal. She gave him a curious stare.

"I'm Lou," she said. "Who are you?"

"Other… I mean, Jack," said Jack.

"What you selling, then?"

"Me? I don't have anything to sell."

"Ah. No money for the merchandise. There's a story I know for sure. That's rough. What about gathering? Windfalls? Cress? Winkles?"

Jack just shook his head.

"Entertainer then?"

"What do you mean?"

The girl frowned. "Juggler? Tumbler? Sing, do you? Punch and Judy show?"

"No, I don't know about any of those."

"Just as well. This isn't the place for that sort of merriment. Well, then, you'll have to have a job."

"I know about being a scullery boy and book-keeping, but I'm not doing that again. That's not my fortune."

The skinny girl laughed. "Not much use here anyway! Minding horses, running messages, sweeping out wagons, loading and unloading — that's what they need hereabouts. Better look sharp."

"I'm Lou," she said. "Who are you?"

Jack didn't know if she was talking to herself or him, but he didn't get a chance to find out.

"Buns, buns, buns!" and she was gone.

Abe returned with a bucket of water and started to unhitch his horse.

"Need a hand?" said Jack.

"Nope," said Abe. "You're done."

Jack picked up his bundle and began to wander around the market. Boots and bells, spices and cloth, perfumes and potions and pancake flippers. The sellers were almost ready, and the buyers were arriving.

Jack stared at the townspeople. They were as clean and polished as schoolteachers. All of them, even the children. The pant legs of the boys went right down to their ankles and no farther. The partings in the girls' hair were as straight as a plow line in a field. Not a rip or a patch or a stain to be seen. Their clothes were sparrow-colored, gray with brown and brown with gray. They spoke in soft voices and not one of them smiled.

"Here!" said a voice. Jack turned around. A woman buried in layers of shawls grabbed his arm in a pinch.

"Mind my patch, will you? Matty's gone off somewheres with her young man and my eggs." She pointed to a faded rag rug on the ground. "Sit there and there's a penny in it for you." Without waiting for a reply she wandered off, muttering something about a "gatless girl."

Jack plunked himself down on the rug. He thought about the penny.

Penny buys a bun! said his stomach. Then he thought about merchandise and pulled out his dictionary. Merchant. Merchandise. Goods, stock, things, stuff. What does a traveler have to sell? What does a traveler make or grow or find or glean?

Ah, well, at the moment he wasn't a merchant but a minder. And there was plenty to look at.

He took a deep breath. Behind it all, behind the horses and the cinnamon and the dust was the smell of the sea, like the blue that lies behind a blue sky.

Sights and sitting, he said to himself. That's the life of a patch minder.

Chapter Ten

"WHAT ARE *you* selling?"

Jack looked up with a start. It was a young woman looking down her nose at him.

"What's your merchandise, sir? Air?"

Jack stared at the young woman. Something in the scorn with which she said "air" reminded him of somebody.

Oh, yes. It was Sophie, one of the big girls at the school. When Sophie was twelve she was apprenticed to a hat-maker. Overnight she changed from a normal human orphan or foundling to a look-down-your-noser Lady Muck, all comments and scorn and la-di-dah ways. She was so full of herself that she hadn't room for one new thought. She was perfect for teasing.

This was another Sophie, right enough.

"I sell whims," he replied.

The young woman wrinkled her nose and put her finger on her chin.

"Whims? That's silly. Who would *buy* a whim?"

"They're bought by people who have run out of whims," said Jack. "People who have used up their whole supply. People whose whims are worn out, or moldy, or out of style."

The young woman frowned. Then she made a little "hnuh" sound in her nose and turned on her heel.

Jack was just about to let out the laugh that was building inside him when she turned back.

"Out of style?"

"Yes," said Jack. "Most people like to replace their whims every season. The better people, anyway."

Jack's customer looked as though she were rooted to the ground. "How much do they cost?"

Jack did some fast thinking. This was better than any Sophie tease.

"One apple."

The young woman's mouth fell slightly open.

"Just a minute."

Jack watched, holding in his giggles, as she went to the fruit barrow across the square. She returned holding a large red apple streaked with gold.

"One whim, please."

Jack and his stomach had a fast little conversation.

It was just supposed to be a joke.

Take that apple!

I'm not really a merchant.

Take that apple!

What if I get in trouble?

Take that apple!

Jack took the apple and gazed out across the market. In the background he heard the rhythmical tap of someone hammering.

"All right," he said. "Here's a whim, latest style. If you glue little pieces of metal to the soles of your shoes, you can make music when you dance."

"But I'm not allowed to dance," protested the young woman.

"Oh, that's all right," said Jack. "You don't have to *do* it. It's just an idea, after all."

"Oh… " said the young woman. "Well, then… " And she wandered away.

The crunch of the apple was like music. The juice ran down Jack's chin, and he could barely chew for laughing.

His life as a minder was cut short, however, by the arrival of the gatless girl's mother, reclaiming her spot. She was laden with eggs and full of a long story about the foolishness of young love. Jack got his penny and went to find Lou. His ears led him straight to her.

Lou gave him the special two-for-a-penny rate

and told him a thing or two about Aberbog while he munched.

"You'd find more lively company in a crew of clams," she said. They don't go in for smiling nor laughing nor passing the time of day. And did you see the over-good children? I don't believe they are children at all. I think they are shrunk-down grown-ups. They don't know what fun is. Last fall the market people got up a bit of a party on the last night of the fair. We went down to the beach and there was music and dancing. And, would you believe it, the mayor of Aberbog — you'll likely see him, he's got a face like a potato — came round and said we were rowdy and made us be quiet."

"Why do you come here, then?"

"Well, they've got lots of money. These Aberbogians, they work hard and they are the saving kind. They buy lots of buns. Can't afford not to come to the Aberbog Fair. Hey! What's up with that stuck-up crew?"

Lou was looking across the market at a group of girls who were staring and pointing in their direction. Jack recognized his whim customer surrounded by others of her ilk.

He shrugged. "Don't know."

"Here's something to look at then," yelled Lou, and she stuck out her tongue. She grabbed Jack's arm. "Come on, you."

Lou found Jack a job with the farrier, holding the horses while the farrier put on their new shoes. For a few hours of horse-holding, Jack earned a hoop of sausage, which he ate on the spot.

Finally in agreement with his stomach, Jack left the fair and made his way down steep, narrow streets to the sea. He stood at the edge of the beach leaning into the small steady wind that blew against him.

It was late afternoon. From all around the bay the fishing boats were heading home. Some had already been pulled up onto the sand, with men beside them packing sails and mending nets. A man in big black boots crunched past Jack. He was carrying two buckets full of slippery silver fish.

Jack hurried down to the water's edge. He squinted as the sun glinted diamonds on the water. Waves rattled the pebbles on the shore. He picked up a handful of crunchy seaweed and shells and sea-smoothed wood from the ribbon of treasures that the tide had left. Even the quiet-loving Aberbogians could not silence the gulls, who wheeled around the incoming boats, screaming.

Jack spent the rest of the day visiting with crabs, collecting shells — each more perfect than the last — counting the colors of sand close up, lassoing boulders with ropes of kelp and soaking his feet in the waves. As the sun did a slow dive, the fishermen went home to their dinners and Jack ate his sausage and read a very good part of R from his dictionary.

He listened to the slap of the waves in the darkness.

Then he curled up under some sails on the dock and listened to the slap of the waves in the darkness. He grinned and wondered what the scornful girl was doing with her whim.

Waves and whims, he said to himself. That's the life of a man of the sea.

Chapter Eleven

MORNING saw Jack trudging back up the hill to the fair. His stomach pronounced a firm NO on seaweed for breakfast. He hoped the farrier needed help again.

No sooner had he stepped into the square, however, than a large woman in a snowy white apron grabbed his arm.

"Here he is," she called.

Everything that Jack had ever done wrong flashed through his mind.

RUN!

But the woman's hand was big and strong.

"Are you the fellow with the whims?" she asked.

Jack gulped.

SAY NO! SAY NO!

But Jack's head nodded.

"Good," said the woman. "It's him," she called out.

A knot of people appeared and surrounded Jack.

"Now, let's get down to business," said the woman. "What have you got today?"

"Um… ideas?" said Jack, his voice cracking a bit.

"Right, then. What sort?"

"Well, I've got whims, of course. And…" Something streaked across Jack's brain, some kind of shooting star of words. "I've got thoughts, concepts, plans, opinions, impressions, notions and fancies."

"How much are impressions?" said the woman.

Breakfast!

"They cost a small round of cheese," said Jack.

"Fair enough," said the woman. "Alice!"

A pale girl appeared. "Cheese, Alice. Small round. Look lively!" Alice sped off.

Jack put his chin on his hand and stared up at the sky. He looked down at the ground. He saw a sprinkling of flour across the woman's sturdy black shoes. Then he stared at the hills behind the town where the morning mist was just starting to burn off.

A panting, pale Alice arrived back carrying a small yellow cheese.

Jack hummed a bit. "One impression. The hill in the middle is a giant carrot pudding just out of the oven."

The woman stared, too.

"Yes," she said. "It is. The very thing."

The woman told her friends and they told their friends and soon there was a steady stream of customers.

The fisherman with the bucket of silvery fish appeared with an identical twin brother. They hung about the edges of the crowd of customers, nudging each other.

"You go, Perkins."

"No, you go, Snik."

Jack remembered Ned at school. Ned could only speak late at night in the dark, when you couldn't look at him.

Carefully looking in the opposite direction from the fishermen, Jack called out, "Special! Ideas special! Notions about the sea! Going fast! Get them while they're hot!"

There was a small cough just over his left shoulder.

"We'll have one," said a voice.

"A well-made one," said another.

"Right," said Jack, addressing the air. "One well-made, fresh, first-class notion about the sea. To a man of the land, seaweed smells like the sea. To a man of the sea, seaweed smells like the land."

"He's right there."

"Dead right."

The day wore on. The line of customers never got shorter. Jack's supply of merchandise never got smaller. All the ideas he had had in the hours scrubbing pots, stirring soup and lying in his bed too cold to sleep. They were all ready and waiting to be custom-made into words and offered for sale. He felt as though he were opening the windows of his head and letting the sun shine in and the breezes blow through.

By evening Jack had had three good meals. His stomach was quieter than it had ever been in his life. He had new boots that were roomy and smooth and hugged his feet softly. He had an umbrella, the promise of a bed at the inn, a whittling knife, a tin cup, a new cap in discreet brown, a bottle of medicine to cure what ails you, a packsack with straps and pockets, a jar full of pennies, a dictionary with all the letters, and his own piece of rug to sit on.

As he began to roll up this rug at the end of the day, he noticed a small pumpkin tart that he had overlooked in the flurry of trading. His stomach suggested that he transport it inside himself, so he popped it in his mouth. It was creamy and spicy and rich.

Plans and pumpkin pie, he said to himself. That's the life of a fellow of fortune.

Chapter Twelve

JACK WAS LATE at the market the next morning because the night before he had discovered an entirely new pleasure. Reading in bed. A full stomach, a soft mattress, a feather comforter, a pillow, a long candle and nobody to tell you what to do. Jack felt that heaven must be something like that. He read his favorite part of the T's, a new part of B and all the words beginning with "ex." He barely had the wits to blow out the candle before he fell asleep.

In the morning he drank coffee for the first time and decided that there was really no need for heaven at all. A line-up had already formed at his spot when he arrived, but he was so full of ham and eggs and coffee and kindness that he decided to begin the day's commerce with free samples for children.

I'm like a Benevolent, he said to himself. I'd better get a hat.

For an hour or so he handed out notions and fancies. Trolls under bridges, rabbits who live on the moon, using a bag of water for a bed, houses made of candy, secret languages, the battle of the cats and the spaniels, ten excellent uses for a piece of string and kingdoms under the sea.

The tidy, pale, polite, over-good children started to talk and laugh, and their parents didn't even seem to mind. In fact the people of Aberbog seemed very different altogether. They were wandering around with little half-smiles on their faces, murmuring things like, "Drawer spelled backwards is reward," and "Maybe the tide doesn't go out. Maybe the land comes in."

Jack was just handing out a notion to a freckled toddler about the surprising things you can bake in a pie when a hush fell over the crowd.

Jack looked up to see a potato-faced man coming his way.

A whisper ran round the crowd. "The mayor, the mayor."

"What are you doing here? What are you selling?" said the mayor. He strode up to Jack, practically knocking over the toddler.

"I'm selling ideas," said Jack. "I'm an ideas peddler, but I'm not quite finished with my customer. Feel free to join the line-up."

But the toddler had begun to cry, and her mother picked her up and swept her away.

"Line-up! Pwah! Where do you get these ideas?"

"I make them," said Jack.

"Sounds like you make them *up*." The mayor's potato face was turning pink.

Jack put his finger on his chin and looked out toward the hills.

"Yes," he said. "Up, down, sideways and through."

There were some giggles from the crowd. The mayor spun around and glared at them.

"All right," he said. "Let's have a look at one of these so-called ideas."

"Thought, concept, plan, opinion, impression, notion, fancy or whim?" inquired Jack.

"Give me a whim," said the mayor, turning pinker.

"Normally," said Jack, "the price for a whim is one apple. But you are one lucky man. This is free sample morning. So here's a whim. If, on a sunny day, you hold your hand like this... " Jack held up his hand with all the fingers together and flat, and the thumb touching the middle finger " ...you can make a shadow that looks like a duck."

The potato turned from pink to purple. The mayor opened and closed his mouth like a fish.

"A duck! What good is that? What's it *for*? What *use* are these ideas?"

Jack spoke very quietly. "The use of them is fresh air for the brain. They make you stop and smile and say to yourself, Gee whillikers, I never thought of that before."

"That's nonsense," said the mayor.

"Not actually," replied Jack. "I don't sell nonsense. That's for the nonsense peddler. He's got all kinds of nonsense — absurdity, folly, trash, moonshine, twaddle, drivel, claptrap, bosh, balderdash, gobbledygook —"

"Quiet," roared the mayor. "Aberbog will not stand for this insolence. You will hear from me tomorrow." And he turned on his heel and stamped off.

Everyone stared at Jack in silence. The children looked scared and pale again. Jack just shrugged.

"I don't think he really liked his whim, do you? Maybe he would have liked the one about jumping frogs instead. What? You don't know about leapfrog? Leapfrog is a very good idea when you're waiting in line. Come on, I'll show you."

Jack organized the small children into a leapfrog line, all the while thinking of Edwin. The mayor was another Edwin. A bully, a basher a...tyrant.

The ways of the world and the ways of school. Not so different after all.

He noticed a timid girl hesitating at the leapfrog line. "Hunker down, everybody. Small one coming."

Leaping to the top of the line successfully, the girl shyly handed Jack a piece of toffee.

Toffee and tyrants, said Jack to himself. That's the life of an ideas peddler.

Chapter Thirteen

IN THE AFTERNOON business was brisk. Townspeople and peddlers alike could not get enough of
Jack's ideas. Some of the wealthier people bought
one of each kind, so Jack had to add new types of
merchandise such as intuitions and hunches.

In addition to the things stuffed into his pack and
a whole basket of food, Jack had promises. Promise
of a day's fishing, promise of a visit to new puppies,
promise of a haircut.

He had just closed up shop to take his first juggling lesson, when loud Lou appeared.

"Emergency," she said. "Come with me. You've
got a problem."

"But I'm just getting the hang of juggling two
oranges. Look."

Lou tugged at his sleeve, making Jack drop both
oranges. "Come *on*. This is important."

Lou led Jack down a road that skirted the top of the town. At the end of the road was a big building with unfriendly windows. Lou led Jack to some bushes that hugged the back of the building.

"Lucky for us it's so hot. They've left one window open. There's a spot there through those bushes where we can spy."

The spot up against the building was dim and dusty and carpeted in dry dead leaves. Both Jack and Lou had to twist their bodies into a half crouch to peek over the windowsill.

Jack peered in and saw a round table ringed by men. He recognized several of his customers. There was the redhead who had bought an opinion on whether sunrise was better than sunset. There was the stuttering man who had purchased a fancy about sneezing.

And there was the potato-faced mayor. He was roaring.

"We have to do something about that ideas peddler down at the market. He is dangerous."

"But… " said a bald man, holding up one finger.

"Yes?" roared the mayor, now a potato of a purple color. "Do you have something to say?"

"Er, no," said the man.

"So, what do we think about these so-called ideas? Eh? Eh? Speak up, everybody. Speak up."

Silence.

"Excuse me, gentlemen." The mayor's voice grew suddenly quiet. "Silent councillors are not useful. Silent councillors are apt to find themselves out of a job."

So one by one they spoke, at first slowly, and then in a chorus.

"New ideas are hazardous and untidy."

"Ideas are noisy."

"They don't match."

"They collect dust."

"They shed."

"They hurt your brain."

"They cause allergies."

The mayor smiled, and his face turned from purple to mauve. "So what should we do with the ideas peddler?"

"Throw him in jail," yelled the councillors in chorus.

"That's it," said the mayor. "And throw away the key. Get the policeman!"

Jack sank back on his heels.

"Come *on*," hissed Lou. "We've got to get out of here."

Lou knew a back route to the market. Over walls, under fences, through a cow field, across a stream on stepping stones. Lou ran like the wind. Jack slipped and stumbled and almost lost his words.

By the time Jack and Lou arrived back at the

market, everyone was talking. Ideas were blowing around like soap bubbles.

"We'll dunk the policeman," said Perkins.

"In the fountain," said Snik.

"Headfirst," said Perkins.

"We'll help," squealed all the formerly well-behaved Aberbog children.

Jack stopped dead in his tracks. It was a hubbub.

His side. Everyone was on his side. His side had always been a small place for one. Now it was big and crowded and noisy.

One of Jack's customers, a wealthy cogitations man, stepped forward and grabbed Jack by the shoulder.

"Gideon. Miller. Pleased to meet you. Now look smart, young fellow. The law is upon us."

He picked up the timid little leapfrog girl. "Hold tight, Christabel."

He set off in a heavy-footed run, Christabel bouncing in his arms and Jack sticking tight. Past the edge of the market and up the hill they came to a large, sturdy wagon. In a flash Jack was heaved into the back, covered with flour sacks and off they went.

After a few minutes Jack felt a weight settle in beside him. A small foot in a clean, soft leather boot wiggled its way under the sack.

"Hold my foot if you're scared," came a whisper.

Jack wasn't exactly scared. He recognized in

Gideon a man who knew how to stay out of trouble. But Christabel's invitation was too kind to refuse. So, joined hand to foot, they wheeled smoothly along the road as the hubbub of the market retreated.

For a time there was only silence and the soft clop of horses on dust. Then there was a rushing sound that got louder and louder. Then the voice of Gideon.

"Home. Safe and sound. Out you come."

Jack popped out from under the sacks and found himself staring at a huge waterwheel turning slowly as rushing water spilled over it. Of course — flour sacks, a waterwheel. Miller was a job, not just a name. Jack jumped down.

The waterwheel was on the side of a big stone building. The building did not have windows, and it looked like a tidy mountain. Next to the mountain was a white-painted house with a wide porch, two cats asleep on the front step — one black, one ginger — and roses growing over the door.

The door opened and out came one of Jack's notions customers — a plump, smiley woman with hair braided on the top of her head.

"Well, if it isn't the Master of Ideas," she said.

"On the lam," said Gideon. "Fugitive from justice. I've offered succor."

Lam. Succor. Jack thought of his dictionary sitting in his pack in the market.

"Well, if it isn't the Master of Ideas."

All of a sudden he felt bereft. Like lonely, but more so. Safe but lost to himself. The sound of the rushing water filled his ears.

Lost and lonely, he said to himself. That's the life of a fugitive from justice.

Chapter Fourteen

As Jack stood in the miller's yard fighting off tears and panic, he felt a little hand slide into his.

"Come on," said Christabel. "I'll show you everything."

"Don't be long," said her mother. "I'm almost serving up."

A quick tour of mill and riverbank and house was accompanied by the ginger cat and continuous description from Christabel. Ginger's kittens. The fairies who live under the rhubarb leaves. The mean village girls who wouldn't play with her.

"All because Mama and Papa came from Fnibble, not Aberbog. They say that people from Fnibble aren't proper."

Jack was amazed at the machinery of the mill. Waterwheel to axel, axel to big gear, big gear to small gear, small gear to stone spindle, stone spindle to millstone.

Wood and stone. Every piece working. Every piece fitting.

Upstream in the millpond there was a small dock. "Come fishing," it whispered.

In the house there were jugs of flowers. Jack had never seen flowers brought inside. What were they for? Just for beauty. The panic in him began to dissolve.

The tour was followed by a meal for which the word dinner did not do justice. Repast, more like it, or feast.

Steaming bowls and jugs and platters made their way around the table in a slow parade of deliciousness. Roast pork, spicy red cabbage, a mashed potato mountain, gravy, chutney, bread and butter. Gradually, food filled in the places where the loneliness had been.

Then the visitors began. At the first knock Gideon hid Jack away. But it was only the spice peddler and Lou with Jack's pack. They were invited to stay for a sip and a bite.

Then a stream of visitors appeared. Townspeople and peddlers, merchants and fishermen.

Over the course of the evening the house filled up. At first the travelers sat on one side of the room and the townspeople on the other — the shy and the stand-offish. But then the pickled-onion peddler took out her fiddle, and the dancing began. What with reels and polkas and the grand chain, everyone got pretty well mixed together. Christabel stuck to Jack's side like glue.

When they rested for cider, there were stories and songs and lots of ideas. The most popular idea, launched by the baker, was that the town should get rid of the mayor.

"Who needs a mayor? We can manage quite well without one."

"Let's persuade him to move along to Sogville."

"Or Bigwick. They would love him in Bigwick."

"Or Mudge-upon-Muddle."

Everybody burst into peals of laughter.

"Serve them right, those stick-in-the-muds."

Jack turned to Lou. "What are they talking about?"

"Oh, those are the towns up and down the coast. Strung out like seawrack, they are."

"What are they like?"

"Like Aberbog, full of house-dwellers. But all different, too. All with their own ways. In Bigwick the women go out fishing. In Mudge there's a house made out of bottles. It makes music on windy nights. It's like… ah, you can't know till you go."

Lou finished the last of her cider. "Grand house this, isn't it?"

"It is that," said Jack.

Lou gave him a hard stare. "I've got something for you, Jack." She leaned over and slipped off one of her shoes. She took from it three small sword-shaped leaves and handed them to Jack.

"What's this?"

"Mugwort. Traveler's herb. Put it in your shoe and you will never tire of walking."

"But what about you?"

Lou grinned. "Don't worry about me. I know where it grows."

When the party finally ended and the last guests dribbled out the door, Mrs. Miller gave Jack a night-shirt and tucked him into a bed by the fire. She put a glass of milk by his bed.

"A little nightcap," she said.

Gideon came to say goodnight. "Could always use a smart lad like you in the mill, apprentice-like," he said. "Think about it. Sleep tight."

Jack lay in the clean warmth.

Food at bedtime, special clothes to wear to bed, someone wishing you goodnight. Those must be family things.

Nightshirts and nightcaps, he said to himself as he dozed off. That's the life of a family man.

Chapter Fifteen

JACK WOKE UP to the merest hint of a gray dawn. He was melting. A nightshirt, a bed with three covers, a cat purring on his chest and a fire at his head, the embers still glowing. He kicked off the covers and gave himself an airing.

Birds were twittering at the window. The kinds of birds that go with roses around the door and a glass of milk at bedtime.

Suddenly their little choir was interrupted by a harsh, screeching cry.

Jack slid out of bed and over to the window just in time to see the departing beat of a seagull. Rude and free and full of opinions.

Jack pushed open the window. A breeze cooled his sweaty curls. The millwheel was at rest.

Turn and grind. Rest. Turn and grind. Rest.

He imagined a splash of water starting in the millpond, dawdling by the fishing dock, then sliding over the milldam, rushing through the millrace, skedaddling through the sluiceway, spilling onto the waterwheel, a fast ride down and then falling back into the river, slowly meandering its way to the sea, its work done.

My work is done, said Jack to himself. They've got their own ideas now. All those plans, hiding and dunking and ditching the mayor. First-class premium ideas. They won't be able to stop now.

I don't like what you're thinking.

Here's what I'm thinking, said Jack. I'm thinking of Sogville and Bigwick and Mudge-upon-Muddle. Fisherwomen and houses that sing. So many places to see. So many roads. I won't know till I go, will I?

Jack pulled his nightshirt over his head, folded it carefully and laid it on the bed. He got dressed and packed his pack.

He opened his old dictionary. "Succor: help in time of need. Seawrack: seaweed and driftwood cast up on the shore by the tide." A settling word and a traveling word. Two bits of Aberbog to take with him on the road.

He left behind the umbrella, most of the food and the medicine for what ails you, because nothing did. He also left behind his new dictionary. His old friend would do fine. He had no need for aggravation and ague or boils and bombardment.

He found a bit of paper on which he wrote, in his best writing, "Thank you. I'll come and visit again.

A traveler." He tucked it in under the empty milk glass and let himself quietly out the door.

NOT EVEN STAYING FOR BREAKFAST?

Jack grinned as he walked down the road toward the sunrise. Down through the forest, through the town. Down past the empty market, down to the sea. Standing on the beach, he settled his pack more comfortably on his shoulders and looked in both directions. A bright mist was rising from the water.

South, he decided. Birds migrate south for the winter.

At the end of the beach, beyond the last fishing boat, another screaming seagull flew low over the pausing boy.

Plop. Jack groaned and took off his cap, crowned with a sloppy white farewell. Shaking his head, he rinsed out his cap in the sea.

Droppings and risings, he said to himself. That's the life of a man of the road.

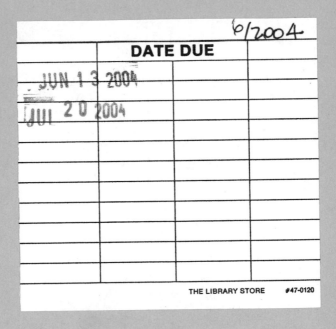